THIS **Elephant & Piggie** BOOK
BELONGS TO:

_____

_____

_____

To Conny and Casey

I Am Invited to a Party!

Mo Willems

WALKER BOOKS
AND SUBSIDIARIES
LONDON · BOSTON · SYDNEY · AUCKLAND

An **Elephant & Piggie** Book

Gerald!

4

I am invited to a party!

It is cool.

Will you go with me?

12

What if it is a fancy party?

We must be ready.

Really?

17

Zip!

Zap!

Zap!

Zip!

A fancy pool party?

He knows
parties.

33

Zip!

Zap!

Zap!

zip!

Zip!

Zap!

Zip!

Well, that is a surprise.

Party!

Mo Willems is the renowned author of many award-winning books, including the Caldecott Honor winners *Don't Let the Pigeon Drive the Bus!*, *Knuffle Bunny* and *Knuffle Bunny Too*. His other groundbreaking picture books include *Knuffle Bunny Free, Leonardo, the Terrible Monster* and *Edwina: The Dinosaur Who Didn't Know She Was Extinct*. Before making picture books, Mo was a writer and animator on Sesame Street, where he won six Emmys. Mo lives with his family in Massachusetts, USA.

Visit him online at **www.mowillems.com** and **www.GoMo.net**

This is a work of fiction. Names, characters, places and incidents are either the product of the author's imagination or, if real, used fictitiously.

First published in Great Britain 2008 by Walker Books Ltd
87 Vauxhall Walk, London SE11 5HJ

First published in the United States by Hyperion Books for Children
British publication rights arranged with Sheldon Fogelman Agency, Inc.

This edition published 2012

6 8 10 9 7

© 2007, 2012 Mo Willems

The right of Mo Willems to be identified as author and illustrator of this work has been asserted by him in accordance with the Copyright, Designs and Patents Act 1988

This book has been typeset in Century 725 and Grilled Cheese

Printed in China

British Library Cataloguing in Publication Data:
a catalogue record for this book is available from the British Library

ISBN 978-1-4063-3843-0

www.walker.co.uk